THIS **ELEPHANT & PIGGIE** BOOK
BELONGS TO:

_____

_____

_____

To Conny and Casey

I Am Invited to a Party!

By Mo Willems

WALKER BOOKS
AND SUBSIDIARIES
LONDON · BOSTON · SYDNEY · AUCKLAND

An **ELEPHANT & PIGGIE** Book

3

I am invited to a party!

Cool.

It is cool.

Will you go with me?

I will go with you.

I *know* parties.

12

What if it is a fancy party?

We must be ready.

Really?

I know parties.

He knows parties.

19

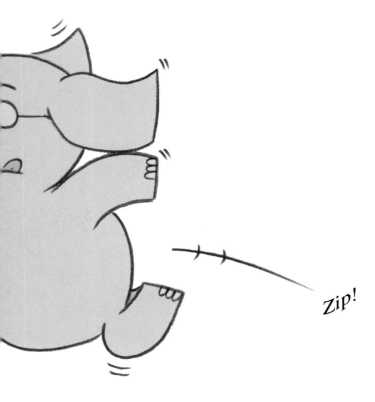

Zip!

Zap!

Zap!

22

Zip!

23

Is this fancy?

VERY FANCY.

26

27

What if it is a pool party?

A fancy pool party?

WE MUST BE READY!!!

I know parties.

He knows
parties.

33

Zip!

Zap!

Zap!

zip!

We will make a splash.

41

Wait!

What if it is a costume party?

45

WE MUST BE READY!!!

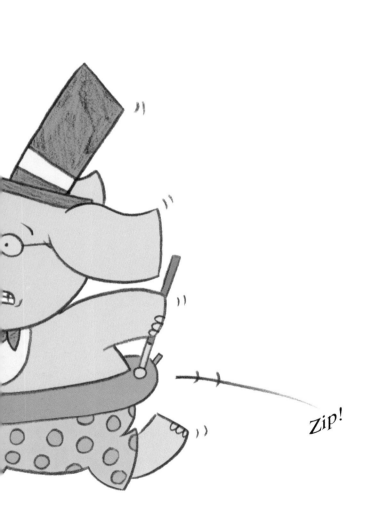

Zip!

He had better
know parties…

Zap!

Zap!

Zip!

Yes. Now we are ready.

Well, that is a surprise.

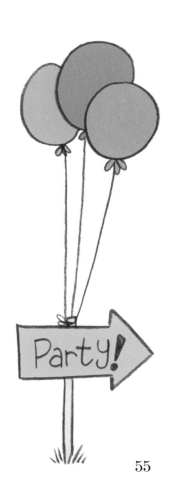

Party!

You *do* know parties!

Mo Willems is the author of the Caldecott Honor-winning books
Knuffle Bunny: A Cautionary Tale and *Don't Let the Pigeon Drive the Bus!*
His other groundbreaking picture books include *Leonardo, the Terrible Monster*
and *Edwina, the Dinosaur Who Didn't Know She Was Extinct.*

Mo began his career as a writer and animator on *Sesame Street*,
where he garnered six Emmy Awards.

First published in Great Britain 2008 by Walker Books Ltd
87 Vauxhall Walk, London SE11 5HJ

2 4 6 8 10 9 7 5 3 1

First published in the United States by Hyperion Books for Children
British publication rights arranged with Sheldon Fogelman Agency, Inc.

This book has been typeset in Century 725 and Grilled Cheese

Printed in Singapore

British Library Cataloguing in Publication Data:
a catalogue record for this book is available from the British Library

ISBN 978-1-4063-1469-4

www.walkerbooks.co.uk

www.pigeonpresents.com

Meet Elephant Gerald and Piggie.

Gerald is careful. Piggie is not.
Piggie cannot help smiling. Gerald can.
Gerald worries so that Piggie does not have to.

Gerald and Piggie are best friends.

In *I Am Invited to a Party!* Piggie is invited to her
first party. But what will she wear? Gerald, the party expert,
knows just how to help … or does he?

The New York Times Book Review says:

"In the world of children's books, the biggest
new talent to emerge thus far in the '00s is
the writer-illustrator Mo Willems."

www.walkerbooks.co.u

ISBN 978-1-4063-1469-4

9 781406 314694 901

£4.99 UK ONLY

KS-788-212